THE CASK
OF AMONTILLADO

*This American classic
is presented without adaptation as part
of the Creative Classic series.*

THE CASK OF AMONTILLADO

EDGAR ALLAN POE

Illustrated by Byron Glaser

Creative Education, Inc.
Mankato, Minnesota

Book Design: Neumeier Design Team

Published by Creative Education, Inc.
123 South Broad Street, Mankato, Minnesota 56001

Library of Congress Cataloging in Publication Data

Poe, Edgar Allan, 1809-1849.
    The cask of Amontillado.

    SUMMARY: After enduring many injuries of the noble Fortunato Montressor executes the
perfect revenge.
    [1. Crime and criminals — Fiction. 2. Horror stories] I. Title.
PZ7.P7515Cas   [Fic]   80-21466
ISBN 0-87191-773-4

To
the continuation of fine literature
for readers of all ages.

THE CASK OF AMONTILLADO
EDGAR ALLAN POE

HE THOUSAND INJURIES
of Fortunato I had borne as I best could, but when
he ventured upon insult I vowed revenge. You, who
so well know the nature of my soul, will not suppose,
however, that I gave utterance to a threat. *At length*
I would be avenged; this was a point definitely
settled — but the very definitiveness with which it was
resolved precluded the idea of risk. I must not only
punish but punish with impunity. A wrong is unredressed when retribution overtakes its redresser. It is
equally unredressed when the avenger fails to make
himself felt as such to him who has done the wrong.

It must be understood that neither by word nor
deed had I given Fortunato cause to doubt my good

will. I continued, as was my wont, to smile in his face, and he did not perceive that my smile *now* was at the thought of his immolation.

He had a weak point — this Fortunato — although in other regards he was a man to be respected and even feared. He prided himself on his connoisseurship in wine. Few Italians have the true virtuoso spirit. For the most part their enthusiasm is adopted to suit the time and opportunity, to practise imposture upon the British and Austrian *millionaires*. In painting and gemmary, Fortunato, like his countrymen, was a quack, but in the matter of old wines he was sincere. In this respect I did not differ from him materially; — I was skilful in the Italian vintages myself, and bought largely whenever I could.

It was about dusk, one evening during the supreme madness of the carnival season, that I encountered my friend. He accosted me with excessive warmth, for he had been drinking much. The man wore motley. He had on a tight-fitting parti-striped dress and his head was surmounted by the conical cap and bells. I was so pleased to see him that I thought I should never have done wringing his hand.

I said to him—"My dear Fortunato, you are luckily met. How remarkably well you are looking today. But I have received a pipe of what passes for Amontillado, and I have my doubts."

"How?" said he. "Amontillado? A pipe? Impossible! And in the middle of the carnival!"

"I have my doubts," I replied; "and I was silly enough to pay the full Amontillado price without consulting you in the matter. You were not to be found, and I was fearful of losing a bargain."

"Amontillado!"

"I have my doubts."

"Amontillado!"

"And I must satisfy them."

"Amontillado!"

"As you are engaged, I am on my way to Luchresi. If any one has a critical turn it is he. He will tell me —"

"Luchresi cannot tell Amontillado from Sherry."

"And yet some fools will have it that his taste is a match for your own."

"Come, let us go."

"Whither?"

"To your vaults."

"My friend, no; I will not impose upon your good nature. I perceive you have an engagement. Luchresi—"

"I have no engagement; — come."

"My friend, no. It is not the engagement, but the severe cold with which I perceive you are afflicted. The vaults are insufferably damp. They are encrusted with nitre."

"Let us go, nevertheless. The cold is merely nothing. Amontillado! You have been imposed upon. And as for Luchresi, he cannot distinguish Sherry from Amontillado."

Thus speaking, Fortunato possessed himself of my arm; and putting on a mask of black silk and drawing a *roquelaure* closely about my person, I suffered him to hurry me to my palazzo.

There were no attendants at home; they had absconded to make merry in honour of the time. I had told them that I should not return until the morning, and had given them explicit orders not to stir from the house. These orders were sufficient, I

I said to him—"My dear Fortunato, you are luckily met. How remarkably well you are looking today."

well knew, to insure their immediate disappearance, one and all, as soon as my back was turned.

I took from their sconces two flambeaux, and giving one to Fortunato, bowed him through several suites of rooms to the archway that led into the vaults. I passed down a long and winding staircase, requesting him to be cautious as he followed. We came at length to the foot of the descent, and stood together upon the damp ground of the catacombs of the Montresors.

The gait of my friend was unsteady, and the bells upon his cap jingled as he strode.

"The pipe," he said.

"It is farther on," said I; "but observe the white web-work which gleams from these cavern walls."

He turned towards me, and looked into my eyes with two filmy orbs that distilled the rheum of intoxication.

"Nitre?" he asked, at length.

"Nitre," I replied. "How long have you had that cough?"

"Ugh! ugh! ugh! —ugh! ugh! ugh! —ugh! ugh! ugh! —ugh! ugh! ugh! —ugh! ugh! ugh!"

My poor friend found it impossible to reply for many minutes.

"It is nothing," he said, at last.

"Come," I said, with decision, "we will go back; your health is precious. You are rich, respected, admired, beloved; you are happy, as once I was. You are a man to be missed. For me it is no matter. We will go back; you will be ill, and I cannot be responsible. Besides, there is Luchresi—"

"Enough," he said; "the cough is a mere nothing; it will not kill me. I shall not die of a cough."

"True—true," I replied; "and, indeed, I had no intention of alarming you unnecessarily—but you should use all proper caution. A draught of this Medoc will defend us from the damps."

Here I knocked off the neck of a bottle which I drew from a long row of its fellows that lay upon the mould.

"Drink," I said, presenting him the wine.

He raised it to his lips with a leer. He paused and nodded to me familiarly, while his bells jingled.

"I drink," he said, "to the buried that repose

around us."

"And I to your long life."

He again took my arm, and we proceeded.

"These vaults," he said,, "are extensive."

"The Montresors," I replied, "were a great and numerous family."

"I forget your arms."

"A huge human foot d'or, in a field azure; the foot crushes a serpent rampant whose fangs are imbedded in the heel."

"And the motto?"

*"Nemo me impune lacessit."**

"Good!" he said.

The wine sparkled in his eyes and the bells jingled. My own fancy grew warm with the Medoc. We had passed through long walls of piled skeletons, with casks and puncheons intermingling, into the inmost recesses of catacombs. I paused again, and this time I made bold to seize Fortunato by an arm above the elbow.

"The nitre!" I said; "see, it increases. It hangs like moss upon the vaults. We are below the river's bed.

*No one attacks me with impunity.

The drops of moisture trickle among the bones. Come, we will go back ere it is too late. Your cough —"

"It is nothing," he said; "let us go on. But first, another draught of the Medoc."

I broke and reached him a flagon of De Grâve. He emptied it at a breath. His eyes flashed with a fierce light. He laughed and threw the bottle upwards with a gesticulation I did not understand.

I looked at him in surprise. He repeated the movement — a grotesque one.

"You do not comprehend?" he said.

"Not I," I replied.

"Then you are not of the brotherhood."

"How?"

"You are not of the masons."

"Yes, yes," I said; "yes, yes."

"You? Impossible! A mason?"

"A mason," I replied.

"A sign," He said, "a sign."

"It is this," I answered, producing from beneath the folds of my *roquelaure* a trowel.

"You jest," he exclaimed, recoiling a few paces.

19

"But let us proceed to the Amontillado."

"Be it so," I said, replacing the tool beneath the cloak and again offering my arm. He leaned upon it heavily. We continued our route in search of the Amontillado. We passed through a range of low arches, descended, passed on, and descending again, arrived at a deep crypt, in which the foulness of the air caused our flambeaux rather to glow than flame.

At the most remote end of the crypt there appeared another less spacious. Its walls had been lined with human remains, piled to the vault overhead, in the fashion of the great catacombs of Paris. Three sides of this interior crypt were still ornamented in this manner. From the fourth side the bones had been thrown down, and lay promiscuously upon the earth, forming at one point a mound of some size. Within the wall thus exposed by the displacing of the bones, we perceived a still interior crypt or recess, in depth about four feet, in width three, in height six or seven. It seemed to have been constructed for no especial use within itself, but formed merely the interval between two of the colossal supports of the roof of the catacombs, and was backed by one of their circumscribing walls of solid granite.

It was in vain that Fortunato, uplifting his dull torch, endeavoured to pry into the depth of the recess. Its termination the feeble light did not enable us to see.

"Proceed," I said; "herein is the Amontillado. As for Luchresi —"

"He is an ignoramus," interrupted my friend, as he stepped unsteadily forward, while I followed immediately at his heels. In an instant he had reached the extremity of the niche, and finding his progess arrested by the rock, stood stupidly bewildered. A moment more and I had fettered him to the granite. In its surface were two iron staples, distant from each other about two feet, horizontally. From one of these depended a short chain, from the other a padlock. Throwing the links about his waist, it was but the work of a few seconds to secure it. He was too much astounded to resist. Withdrawing the key I stepped back from the recess.

"Pass your hand," I said, "over the wall; you cannot help feeling the nitre. Indeed, it is *very* damp. Once more let me *implore* you to return. No? Then I must positively leave you. But I must first render you all the little attentions in my power."

"The Amontillado!" ejaculated my friend, not yet recovered from his astonishment.

"True," I replied; "the Amontillado."

As I said these words I busied myself among the pile of bones of which I have before spoken. Throwing them aside, I soon uncovered a quantity of building stone and mortar. With these materials and with the aid of my trowel, I began vigorously to wall up the entrance of the niche.

I had scarcely laid the first tier of the masonry when I discovered that the intoxication of Fortunato had in a great measure worn off. The earliest indication I had of this was a low moaning cry from the depth of the recess. It was *not* the cry of a drunken man. There was then a long and obstinate silence. I laid the second tier, and the third, and the fourth,and then I heard the furious vibrations of the chain. The noise lasted for several minutes, during which, that I might hearken to it with the more satisfaction, I

A succession of loud and shrill screams, bursting suddenly from the throat of the chained form, seemed to thrust me violently back.

ceased my labors and sat down upon the bones. When at last the clanking subsided, I resumed the trowel, and finished without interruption the fifth, the sixth, and the seventh tier. The wall was now nearly upon a level with my breast. I again paused, and holding the flambeaux over the mason-work, threw a few feeble rays upon the figure within.

A succession of loud and shrill screams, bursting suddenly from the throat of the chained form, seemed to thrust me violently back. For a brief moment I hesitated, I trembled. Unsheathing my rapier, I began to grope with it about the recess; but the thought of an instant reassured me. I placed my hand upon the solid fabric of the catacombs, and felt satisfied. I reapproached the wall; I replied to the yells of him who clamoured. I re-echoed, I aided, I surpassed them in volume and in strength. I did this, and the clamourer grew still.

It was now midnight, and my task was drawing to a close. I had completed the eighth, the ninth and the tenth tier. I had finished a portion of the last and the eleventh; there remained but a single stone to be fitted and plastered in. I struggled with its weight; I placed it partially in its destined position. But now there came from out the niche a low laugh that erected the hairs upon my head. It was succeeded by a sad voice, which I had difficulty in recognizing as that of the noble Fortunato. The voice said —

"Ha! ha! ha! — he! he! he! — a very good joke, indeed — an excellent jest. We shall have many a rich laugh about it at the palazzo — he! he! he! — over our wine — he! he! he!"

"The Amontillado!" I said.

"He! he! he! — he! he! he! — yes, the Amontillado. But is it not getting late? Will not they be awaiting us at the palazzo, the Lady Fortunato and the rest? Let us be gone."

"Yes," I said,, "let us be gone."

"For the love of God, Montresor!"

"Yes," I said, "for the love of God!"

But to these words I hearkened in vain for a reply. I grew impatient. I called aloud —

"Fortunato!"

No answer. I called again, —

"Fortunato!"

No answer still. I thrust a torch through the remaining aperture and let it fall within. There came forth in return only a jingling of the bells. My heart grew sick; it was the dampness of the catacombs that made it so. I hastened to make an end of my labour. I forced the last stone into its position; I plastered it up. Against the new masonry I re-erected the old rampart of bones. For the half of a century no mortal has disturbed them. *In pace requiescat!*

Edgar Allan Poe
1809-1849

28

EDGAR ALLAN POE, one of America's most imaginative writers, died forgotten and penniless — just as he had lived. From his birth on January 19, 1809, Edgar had to face life's harshest realities. His father, David Poe, died when he was a year and a half. His mother, Elizabeth Arnold Poe, whom he was devoted to, died when Edgar was nearly four.

Elizabeth had been an actress, and Edgar had watched her "die" on stage many times. When tuberculosis took her life at age 24, young Edgar wondered if she were just performing. Death never seemed far from him and those he loved. At age six, Edgar was riding a horse with his foster father, John Allan. As they neared the cemetery, Edgar was seized with terror and screamed, "They will run after us and drag me down."

Edgar's foster father, a severe and stingy man, caused Edgar pain all his life. His foster mother, however, dearly loved him. But she, like his own mother, was sick most of the time Edgar lived with the Allans.

At eight, Edgar went with the Allans to England

and Scotland where he attended all-male schools. While he did well with his studies, Edgar found them stark, hard environments. Yet the influence of French and German, which he studied in these schools, showed up later in his writing. These influences made Poe's style a little different from other American writers.

Back in America, 20-year-old Edgar continued to face obstacles. His foster father sent him to an expensive University but with only a third of the money he'd need. Eventually, Edgar had to quit because of lack of money. Then he fell in love with a woman named Elmira. But, while he was in the Army, he discovered that her father had intercepted all his letters, and Elmira became engaged to another man.

By age 24, Poe had written eleven stories. One of them, "MS Found In A Bottle," won the first prize of 50 dollars in a magazine contest. While magazine publishers bought some of Poe's stories, few trusted Edgar enough to give him steady work as an editor. So Edgar was always scrambling for money.

In 1836, Edgar married his 14-year-old cousin Virginia. And in 1839, a publishing house at last agreed to publish a small edition of his tales in two volumes. Edgar felt his luck had begun to change. Over the next few years, Edgar wrote most of the stories he later became famous for—"The Gold Bug," "The Pit and the Pendulum," and "The Tell-Tale Heart." In 1844, the poem he worked on for ten years—"The Raven"—was published.

Then, just as abruptly, Edgar's luck turned again. Early in 1847, Virginia died, and Poe became unconsolable. The only thing he wrote that year was "Ulalume." After a couple unsuccessful attempts to marry, Poe drank himself into a kind of madness and died October 7, 1849. He was forty years old.

Without a penny to his name, Poe left a rich legacy in his timeless tales and tantalizing poems. His sense of another world came alive under his pen and still haunts millions of readers today.